THE HORSE AND THE MAN
A SHORT STORY

Podium Press

Boulder, Colorado 80306

www.goldmedalmind.com

Printed in the USA

To Dennis and George, whose loyalty and loving guidance allowed me to become more "horselike" than I ever imagined possible. I love the heck out of you.

THE HORSE AND THE MAN: A SHORT STORY

One day a man was racing down a country road in his new sport utility vehicle. He was trying to get back to the city for a number of important reasons. His SUV was complete with cell phone, pager, fax, navigation, heated seats, Bluetooth, bike rack, ski rack, and other modern conveniences. Then, "Boom!" His right rear tire blew out. Luckily, the man regained control of the vehicle, avoiding a crash. He pulled off to the side of the road.

Without questioning his safety, the man jumped out of the vehicle and kicked the tire in anger. Then he cursed at a horse that stood staring at him in the nearby field. He looked up to the sky, asking, "Why, why now? Why me?" Me against the world, as usual, thought the man.

Before he even started looking for a jack, he recalled that he had not had time to pick it up from his brother before leaving on this trip. His brother had borrowed it a year ago and never returned it. The man pictured the jack hanging in his brother's garage, and his anger intensified.

"Damn," yelled the man. "I never have time. I'm so busy!"

This led to a rush of thoughts the man would have preferred to block out. He remembered the time his engine seized because he was too busy to have an oil leak fixed. Strange, he hounded his sons about checking the oil and not letting the gas gauge fall below a quarter-tank, but his own engine seized because he had no time to check the oil! He was reminded of the time when he had to have a second shoulder surgery because he refused to complete the physical therapy his doctor prescribed. He was too busy. And here he was again, in the same place with different circumstances. As usual, he vowed to himself that this would never happen again.

After another glance up to the sky, the man vigorously tore his vehicle apart in search of the jack he knew was not there. As he rifled through his SUV, he began talking to himself—or rather, angrily muttering, the way he always did after making a bad golf shot, losing a business contract, or even after his wife asked to spend more time together.

The man continued his tantrum. The horse calmly watched.

Suddenly, the man went on another tirade. "Where are my cigarettes?" As if blaming some cosmic force, he screamed, "What did you do with them?"

The horse calmly watched.

The man surrendered to the fact that he could not find the jack, because his head was now filled with thoughts of how much better the situation would be if he had a cigarette in hand. His lungs and brain could almost feel the sensation of relief, the rush of nicotine as it coursed through his blood. By this time, his hands were shaking and droplets of perspiration appeared on his face. He almost forgot about the tire as his yen for a smoke consumed him.

The horse calmly watched him.

He glared at the animal and screamed, "Horse, what are you looking at? You stupid animal! Go eat some grass! I'm not crazy, if that's what you're thinking!"

The horse calmly watched him.

Strangely, the horse's quiet gaze reminded the man of his children's faces around the dinner table, watching him while he ranted about world affairs, politics, and taxes. Although the man had immigrated to the United States, was welcomed there, and embraced the opportunity to prosper, he never thought to give thanks. Instead, he took every chance he got to devalue the American way, scoffing, "Baseball, hot dogs, apple pie, and Chevrolet."

The horse began to wonder about this man. Did he have children? Did he take them to the zoo? Did he share the wonders of the animal kingdom with them?

The man's dinner table goal was to convince his wife and children that he knew what was in their best interests. In the man's mind, his family's silence and unresponsive gaze was a sign they agreed with him. He held forth on the stupidity of the welfare system, the weakness of democracy, the apathy of the younger generation, and the unfairness of taxes. "It's a dog-eat-dog world" was his mantra.

When his 16-year-old son was arrested for drunk driving and possession of drugs, the man blamed the school system. After all, if he was going to pay for private education, the school should have done more to keep an eye on the kid. Hypocritically, he became incensed when he thought teachers were acting like parents. He believed firmly they should stick to academics. If his teenage daughter had become pregnant, he would have blamed the school for not providing better sex education. Sex! A taboo topic!

As he rummaged around searching for his cigarettes, muttering to himself, the man remembered a visit he had with his father in the VA hospital's alcohol treatment unit. His father was adamant that his enlarged liver was the fault of the doctors for giving him the wrong medication. Recalling this, the man became agitated, and then pissed off because of how much he spent for counseling so he would not be like his father. He knew that if he were in his father's shoes, he would have blamed the doctors as well.

The horse calmly watched.

Finally, the man gave up looking for his cigarettes and dialed AAA on his cell phone. He yelled, "Hurry! This is urgent. I pay good money for this service!"

After signing off, he shook his head, looked at the horse, and screamed, "What the hell are you looking at?"

The horse sauntered over to the fence and gazed at the man.

The man demanded, "Can you believe this mess? Why now? Why me? I'm busy; I have no time for this." Pausing, the man glared at the horse and screamed, "Would you stop staring and say something!"

"A bit angry, aren't you?" exclaimed the horse.

The man jumped back, startled, and did a double take. He asked himself, "Holy smokes, am I hallucinating?"

The horse said, "Man, what's the rush?"

In spite of himself, the man found himself replying. "I have to get back to the city."

"Why so fast?" asked the horse.

The man retorted, "Golf, contracts, big money...I'm a busy man!"

The horse, not understanding, chose to be quiet. From the horse's perspective, the man should enjoy the moment and the countryside, accept the flat tire, and slow down.

The man looked at his watch and yelled, "Where are they? I'm a busy man. I have no time to wait."

The horse calmly looked at the man, tilted her head and swung her tail from side to side.

The man then stated, "Horse, don't give me that. Be grateful someone is talking to you. Does anyone just stop to chat with a horse?"

"Well, since you asked. Once in a while travelers stop to take a picture of me. I love posing. One time a man gave his kids six minutes to visit with me while he madly flipped through a vacation guidebook. You should have heard those kids. 'Dad is nutso on these trips,' said the girl. The boy said, 'Yeah, I'd rather stay home and not go on these dumb family outings.' Then the girl noticed I could hear them and said, 'Look, the horse is listening! She's nodding. She understands.' But before I could stretch out my nose to touch her hand, the father screamed, 'YOU HAVE 30 SECONDS to get in this car!' and that was that."

The man, growing restless with this tale, interrupted, "Horse, it's easy for you. All you do is stand in your field and do nothing all day. Do you even know what it means to compete in the world?"

Feeling like the man was heating up for an argument, the horse replied, "I get the impression you think I choose to be here chewing grass and sleeping all day!"

It was the man's turn to tilt his head and wonder, "Where else would you want to be?"

"Back on the plains with my family," exclaimed the horse.

The man was beginning to think that he was truly starting to lose his mind. Nevertheless, he asked, "Family! What family?"

The horse began to tell a story of being taken captive and brought to a small town to work for an animal ride in a carnival. She remembered vividly that she had wandered off looking for a fresh water supply, telling her children she would return. Then there was the sting of a tranquilizer gun, and her next memory was waking up in a stable with a bridle tethering her to a post. Three years had passed since she had seen her children.

The man was moved, but stoically refrained from giving in. "Horse, this is crazy. I am feeling sorry for you. But you are only a horse." This was too much for the man. He realized he saw his kids and wife daily, but was actually absent, and not because of a tranquilizer gun. The man screamed, "What is wrong with me!"

The horse calmly watched.

After a long pause, the man decided he really didn't want to be standing there listening to a horse anyway. Why should he care what it had to say? Everyone had problems. He felt a nagging sadness over the horse's story. But in his mind, the past was the past. The horse should just get over it and forget. The man failed to realize that the horse was not bemoaning her fate; she was just telling the man how she came to be in the corral.

Feeling annoyed and agitated, the man automatically reached into his shirt pocket, and there were his cigarettes. "See what you've done, horse! It's your fault I found my cigarettes. I'm trying to quit and now here I go again."

"Quit? Why?" asked the horse.

The man replied, "Doctor's orders." The horse calmly watched the man.

Suddenly, the man looked forlorn. "Look horse, if the damn tire was good, or if I had a jack like I'm supposed to, I wouldn't be having a conversation with a horse. You remind me of the therapist I saw after my second wife left me." He thought for a minute. "She would let me rant, but never assure me it was not my fault my wife had left. It was not helpful. Like you, horse! You are not helpful!"

The horse calmly watched the man, wondering how many times he had been married.

True to character, to steer away from difficult memories, the man blurted out, "So when did you learn to talk?"

"When I stopped trying," replied the horse.

"What!" exclaimed the man. "Are you crazy? Don't give me that yin-yang, Zen crap!"

"I'm not. I'm simply answering your question." The horse continued, "I tried and tried, and then, when I stopped trying, it just happened!"

The man looked down and shook his head. "You sound like these tapes I listened to for my golf game. The ones that tell you to let go, don't try so hard, don't think, be in the moment, one stroke at a time, no judgments, blah, blah, blah."

The horse stated, "It has been the greatest lesson I have learned."

"What, learning to talk?" the man said sarcastically. He was feeling annoyed again.

The horse explained, "I practically died of starvation a year ago. When I was taken from my family, I was so despondent. I didn't want to eat. Seeing children made me even more sad and lonely. One day it occurred to me that I might die, and then I would never be reunited with my family. I had to accept the fact that I was not with them. I had to let go of my sadness and eat to be healthy in case one day I could see them again. I had two choices. One was to stay sad and angry and starve to death. The other was to choose to accept what happened and, perhaps, try to appreciate what I had left. And eventually, to try to help others be happy."

This was just too much. The man turned away, saying, "Horse, I'm happy for you, but I am a busy man." With that, he redialed his phone and yelled, "How long does it take for you people to get here. I pay good money for this road service. I don't have all day!"

The man signed off and lit another cigarette. He paced along the road, smoking furiously.

The horse watched the man for a while, and then turned her attention to the sunset.

The tow truck arrived. The man was relieved. The horse looked at the sunset.

The driver stepped down from the cab and saw the horse. "What a beautiful horse!" he said. "How peaceful she looks."

The man, ready to explode, stated firmly, "Would you kindly fix the tire. I am in a rush."

"Boy, that really is a beautiful horse!" the tow truck driver repeated.

"Yeah, yeah!" agreed the man. "But please fix the damn tire!"

The man thought about his conversation with the horse. Would the driver believe him? No way! Just get the tire done so I can get back to the city, he thought.

The driver returned to his truck and emerged with something in his hand. "I have some sugar packets left over from my coffee. Maybe she will like them." He went over to pet the horse. "I love animals. When I was a kid, my dad never had time to take me to the zoo or teach me about animals," he told the horse.

The man was starting to feel overwhelmed. First the horse, now the driver! "I need a drink!" he screamed.

The driver started changing the tire as the man fired off a flurry of questions. "How far to the next gas station? How long will it take to get to the city on the interstate? Should I take back roads? Can you bill me?"

The tow truck driver was not listening. He continued working and talking to the horse.

The man gave up trying to talk to the driver. Suddenly, he felt sadder than he had for a long, long time. Thinking about all this love, the horse and her family, those kids and the horse, and now the tow truck driver and the horse, triggered feelings of emptiness the man worked hard to keep a lid on.

"Sir, it's finished. Have a safe journey," announced the driver.

Climbing into the SUV, the man expressed his appreciation briefly. "Good day, sir!"

The horse watched the man leave, licking the remnants of sugar off her lips.

The man slammed on the gas to make up for lost time. Then, suddenly, he stopped. He backed up, jumped out with his camera, took a picture of the horse, and smiled. He got back in his car and drove off.

The horse calmly watched the man drive away.

The End

REFLECTION QUESTIONS FOR
"THE HORSE AND THE MAN"

1. What was it like for you to read this story? What thoughts and feelings did you experience?

2. Did the story leave you with questions? What are they?

3. What aspects of the story had the biggest impact on you? Explain why.

4. Have you ever had an experience (either as an athlete or in the game of life) in which your actions and reactions resembled those of the man in the story? How about experiences in which you were more like the horse?

5. Identify and describe three people you know who are more like the man, and three who are more like the horse.

6. Do you see any similarities between the horse's attitude and the gold-medal-mind approach to sport and life?

7. Are there areas in your life where you would like to be more horselike? What would you do differently?

8. Identify and describe any beliefs you may have that a horselike approach to life just will not cut it. For example, do you think that a horse-like approach to meeting a challenge might lack the intensity, fight, drive, or persistence needed to succeed, on or off the field? If so, how come?

9. Describe times in your life as an athlete when you were more like the man. How well did you perform in that state of mind?

10. Do you see a relationship between the man's approach to life and five-ring fever? What is it?

11. Describe your reaction to an event like getting a flat tire, finding a parking ticket on your windshield, or seeing someone zip in front of you and take your parking space.

12. A year had passed and the man was still too busy to go to pick up the jack he had loaned his brother. Are you aware of areas in your life you may be neglecting as a result of being too busy? What are they?

13. To help manage his emotions, the man furiously smoked cigarettes and later craved a drink. What do you do to help yourself feel better when you are experiencing uncomfortable emotions? How well do your strategies work?

14. Why do you think the man became so angry at the horse while the horse remained quiet and calm, simply watching the man?

15. When the horse told the story of how she ended up in the field, the man became sad. Why do you think he felt sad? How did you feel upon hearing that story?

16. The horse shared with the man that she almost died from not eating, only to realize if she died she would never have the chance to reunite with her children. How might you explain the man's reaction to that story? What was your reaction?

17. Have you ever been at a crossroad where negative emotions pulled you to act in a self-destructive way? What happened? Did anything you did or thought help you remain on a healthier path?

18. How do you think the man might be "starving himself" to the point of losing his relationship with his current wife and kids? Do you think he will change based on his encounter with the horse? Why or why not?

19. Do any aspects of the story lead you to believe the man will change for the better based upon his experience with the horse?

20. What aspects of the story lead you to believe the man is unlikely to change as a result of his experience with the horse?

21. Think of the people who you know who are more like the man. Have they tried to change? What approaches have they tried? How well did it work?

22. For a person like the man in the story, what difference would changing make versus not changing? How about an athlete who changes and becomes psychologically skilled versus one who does not?

23. Immediately upon seeing the horse, the tow truck driver went over to give her some sugar, in spite of the fact the man made it clear he was the priority. Describe a few times in your life when you stopped to "feed the horse sugar." Describe times when you had the chance to slow down, but instead marched to the beat of your urgency drum.

24. At the end of the story, when the man started speeding away but instead stopped and took a picture of the horse, what do you think was going on in his mind? What do you think he might do with that picture?

25. We know the horse loved to have her picture taken. When she saw the man stop and take her picture, what thoughts do you imagine she might have had?

26. If you were able to rewrite the ending of the story, what would you change?

27. Is there anyone in your life who you feel might benefit from reading this story? For each person you think of, describe how you think they would benefit.

THE ORIGIN OF *"THE HORSE AND THE MAN"*

Labor Day 1997 was quickly approaching. It was Thursday night, and I was lying in my hammock on my balcony overlooking the city of Denver. My gut was telling me to leave town for the weekend. I just had this heartfelt sense. Where should I go? Lost for an answer to that question, I flipped through *Westword,* a local newspaper that listed all the restaurants, movies, and entertainment for the week. Throughout the summer, large music festivals take place most weekends in Colorado. So I was not surprised to see an announcement for the One World Music Festival in Crested Butte, Colorado. At the time, Crested Butte was still a small ski town about four hours from Denver. I had never been, but the place spoke to me. I knew a handful of the bands scheduled to play at the festival, but was even more intrigued by this small town and the idea of dancing outside for hours on end as if no one were watching.

I was working at Denver Health Medical Center at the time, and we worked a half-day on Friday. I had thrown a bunch of stuff in the car so I could leave right after work. The car I was driving was a 1987

Mercury Topaz, black with an FM radio and cassette player. The bumper was held on securely with duct tape, and red tape effectively covered most of the taillights, given the bumps and bruises the bumper had suffered. I was particularly proud of the fact that the engine was sealed with road grime.

Yes, I had had a slow oil leak for months on end. When I went to the garage hoping for an easy fix, the mechanic informed me that the entire engine would need to be steam cleaned to reveal the leak before he could repair it. His conclusion: "I don't know what we will find. Right now, you have a great seal made of road grime. We clean that engine and you could have a world of hurt on your hands. I would leave it alone, check the oil frequently, and add oil as needed." I had arrived. Thirty-three years old, eight years of graduate school, postdoctoral training at Stanford University School of Medicine, and my car engine was sealed with road grime. I picked up several quarts of oil for my adventure.

I think the desire and urge to escape from the city had something to do with jitters I was feeling. This was the first Labor Day since 1976 that I was clean and sober. Like all holidays, it provided more than a good excuse to celebrate. By the time I got sober, Monday was as good a day as any for me to "celebrate." In fact, any time was a good time to celebrate, whether raining, snowing, sunny, windy, daytime, or nighttime. Thus a holiday weekend typically was a time to take the ongoing party to the next level—especially Labor

Day weekend, as it symbolized the end of summer. I felt a need to do my own thing. I would journey out solo to see what I could find. I would be anonymous. There was something peaceful in the idea of being a stranger, having no expectations of myself and no need to perform.

While on Cottonwood Pass, a two-lane dirt road extending from Buena Vista to Almont, Colorado, I found myself passing horses. Horses were meandering in the fields behind fences, grazing, sunning, and enjoying a cool breeze, by the looks of it. I was driving about 5 mph to take it all in and noticed some of the horses looking up at me as I drove by. The air conditioning was not working, so my windows were down, and I was blasting either the Allman Brothers or Led Zeppelin. Maybe these horses are rock and roll fans, I thought to myself. That's why they are looking at me. After a while I slowed down even more, until I was rolling along the gravel surface mesmerized by the horses. At one point, I turned off the music to take in all the sounds that were stimulating my senses.

As I drove, images started to come to consciousness of a man talking to the horses. It was strange. I continued to drive, gazing at the horses, as my mind's eye saw a conversation ensue between the man and the horses. Given the onslaught of images, I had to keep stopping to scribble my thoughts on whatever I could find—a napkin, scrap pieces of paper, blank pages of books. I can't remember how many times I stopped and started. I knew I was adding time to my journey. But it did not bother me. The idea I would arrive later than originally expected did not faze me. This was a significant departure from the past, when I seemed always to have to get wherever I was going at warp speed.

At some point, my ideas and scribbling came to an end. There I was, sitting in the dirt looking at these animals, in awe of their magnificence. I started talking to them. I had never ridden a horse. I couldn't recall having been around many of them, so what was my fascination? Later, I came to realize the horse symbolized something that always eluded me, in spite of what I achieved professionally. What I was missing were feelings of peace, calm, serenity, security, well being, and self-worth. However, I had no clue about any of this at the time.

Upon pulling into Crested Butte, I found a small mom-and-pop grocery store and bought a pad of paper and an iced tea. I sat on a bench outside the grocery store and put all my pieces of scrap paper in order. As I wrote, the story spontaneously came to life. The last thing I expected when I planned my getaway was to end up talking to horses and sitting on a bench writing about them. But there I was.

The three days at the One World Music Festival turned out to be magical. The bands played from noon to 11 p.m. Saturday and Sunday and noon to 7 p.m. on Monday. The stage was at the base of the mountain, leaving enough room for a healthy-sized dance floor. People were scattered about on the mountainside. I situated myself in the last row at the top, which gave me a total view of the scene. The firewater (a.k.a. booze), weed, and other sorts of mood-altering substances were present in abundance. You would think it would be the perfect invitation for me to join in. There I was, all by myself. No one would know. But I did not have the yen. A feeling of peace filled my body—the same peace I felt while mesmerized by the horses.

As I drove back to Denver Monday night, I stopped in a small town for a bite to eat. While sitting at the counter, I read the story a few times and thought to myself, maybe this is a children's book. It seemed it might be, given that a horse was the main character. But I had not a clue. It felt meaningful, but I had no real connection to the story and no inkling about what it would ultimately reveal to me about myself. Upon returning to Denver, I typed it up as a Word document, printed it out, and put it in an orange folder that followed me around on my journey. I still have this folder, filled with the poetry I wrote during my early days of recovery. It seemed to be the logical place for the story to live.

Fast forward to 2016. I was getting close to finishing my book *The Gold Medal Mind: Becoming a Psychologically Skilled Athlete* and its companion workbook. I considered including some of my poetry in the workbook, as it related to athletics, achievement, competition, victory, defeat, identity, loss, joy, and sadness, all topics I discuss in *The Gold Medal Mind*. That is when I rediscovered the short story. I pushed back from my desk, turned up the music, and read what I had written during my road trip. Tears came to my eyes as I realized what the story was about on a symbolic level. I read it over and over, shaking my head in disbelief that when I wrote it, I had no clue what the story meant. But now it was clear that it captured the transition I ultimately would make—from mindlessly racing around like the man in the story to being more "horse-like" than I ever imagined was possible.

This realization was sweeter than any moment I had as a competitive athlete or coach at the collegiate level.

The experience was surreal. I accepted it as a spiritual experience that resulted from being relieved of what is called "the bondage of self." I thought about how much better I would have been as an athlete if I had been more horselike at the time. That was the inspiration I needed to launch this story with *The Gold Medal Mind*. The horse in the story provides a clear example of what it means to be psychologically skilled. But more importantly, the message of the story applies to the game of life, because there is a little man and a little horse in every one of us.

My hope is that you will relate to the story, spend time with the questions for reflection, and then get in the "locker room" and share your reflections with others. I would be thrilled to know what you discovered about yourself, others, and the world as we know it.

Made in the USA
Monee, IL
21 April 2021

65356828R00020